Fortunately

Valerie Harrigan

Illustrated by Valerie Harrigan & S. Neptune

Copyright © 2013 Valerie Harrigan
All Rights Reserved.

Acknowledgements

Valerie would like to thank her parents, sisters and brother, grandparents, along with her extended family (friends) for their continued support. Her teachers who have inspired her love of reading and writing: Ms. Arika Myles, Mrs. Robin Dennis, Mrs. Linda Wolpert, Ms. Angela Buckler, Mrs. Roberta Blasdell, and Mrs. Sue Thomas. A special thanks to Principal Donna Koval, Mrs. Lynn Clements, and the entire staff of Southern Elementary School in Glen Rock, Pennsylvania.

A tremendous gratitude of thanks to Dr. Demi Stevens, Director of the Paul Smith Library in Shrewsbury, Pennsylvania, and library staff for all of the help and encouragement.

And to all friends and family, dream big.

*To Mrs. Becky
Love
Val*

Fortunately, I found a coupon for a purple and blue saxophone.

Unfortunately, the store owner said the coupon expired yesterday.

Errol's Music Shop
Win a Free Saxophone
Lessons Available
Gift Certificates Available
Sorry dear
SHEET Music

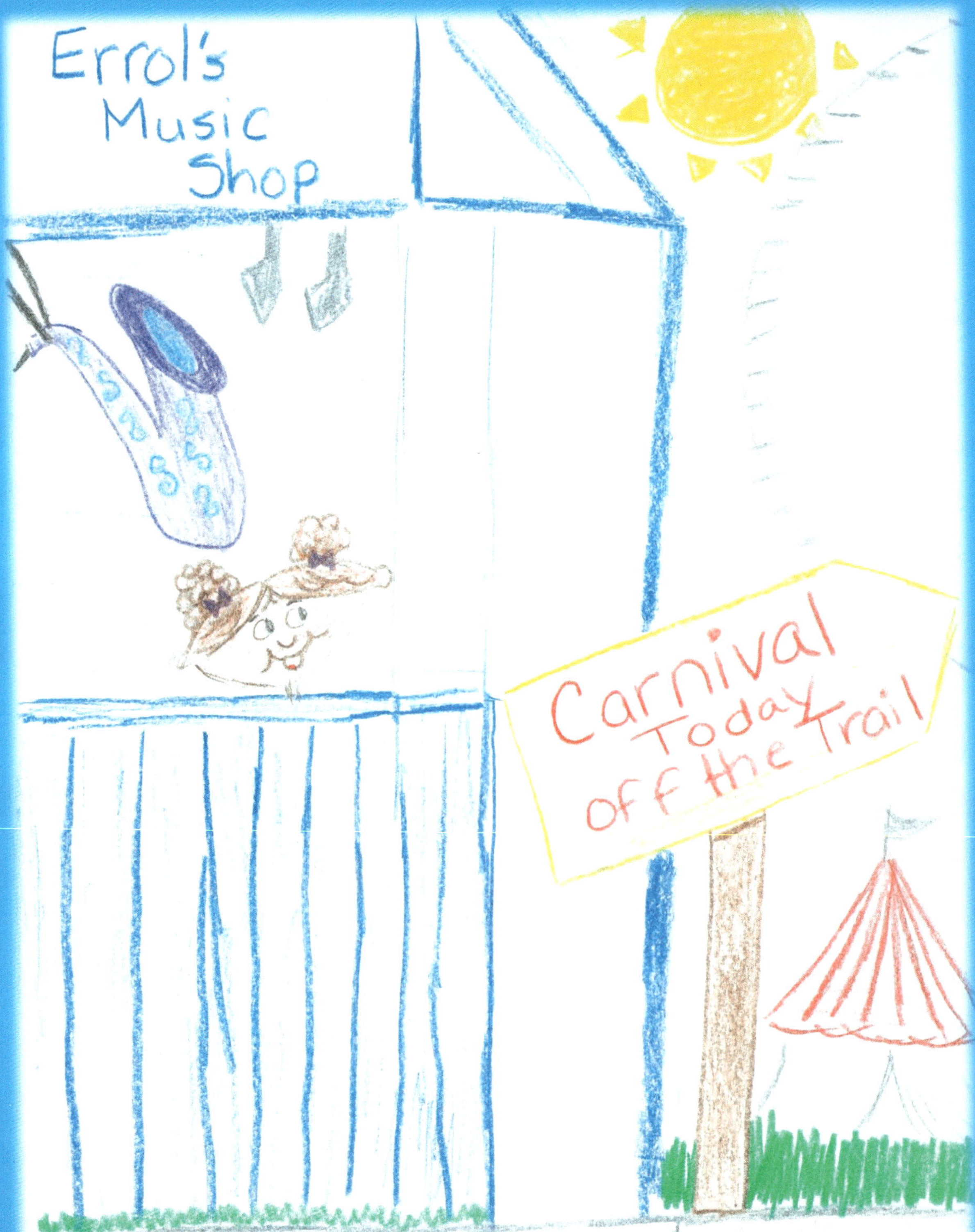
Errol's Music Shop
Carnival Today off the Trail

Fortunately, I saw a sign beside the store pointing to the carnival.

Unfortunately, on one of the rides I almost got struck by lightning!

Fortunately, I got off safely.

Unfortunately, I tripped and fell.

Fortunately, I looked up and saw a beanbag in the shape of a tiger.

Come Meet Tiffany the Tiger

← Glass Enclosure on the opposite side.

Unfortunately, the tiger was real.

Fortunately, I managed to get away.

SES Book Club
Fundraiser

Unfortunately, a thunderstorm rolled in.

Fortunately, I found a shelter

to wait out the storm.

Kitty Palace

Adopt a Kitty Today!!

Aaaaa-chooo

Unfortunately, the shelter was filled with cats.

That made me sneeze!

Fortunately, I sneezed so hard, the force of my sneeze sent me back to the music store.

SHEL
and
RESCU

ADOPT a Pretty Kitty

OPEN

To my amazement, the owner gave me that purple and blue saxophone I had wanted.

That made me happy!